EDGAR GETS READY FOR BED

For my dad, the best storyteller of all. —J. A.

For Keegan and Finley, fly little birds! —R. S.

First Edition
18 17 16 15 14   5 4 3
BabyLit® is a registered trademark of Gibbs Smith, Inc. © 2014, all rights reserved.
BabyLit® brand created by Suzanne Gibbs Taylor for Gibbs Smith.
Text © 2014 Jennifer Adams
Illustrations © 2014 Ron Stucki

Published by
Gibbs Smith
P.O. Box 667
Layton, Utah 84041

1.800.835.4993 orders
www.gibbs-smith.com

Designed and illustrated by Ron Stucki
Printed and bound in China
Gibbs Smith books are printed on either recycled, 100% post-consumer waste,
FSC-certified papers or on paper produced from a 100% certified sustainable
forest/controlled wood source.

Library of Congress Cataloging-in-Publication Data

Adams, Jennifer, 1970-
   Edgar gets ready for bed : a BabyLit first steps book / by Jennifer Adams ; illustrated by Ron
Stucki. — First edition.
       pages cm.
   Summary: "Meet the plucky toddler Edgar the raven. He's mischievous, disobedient, and contrary.
He's also lovable. Inspired by Edgar Allen Poe"— Provided by publisher.
   ISBN 978-1-4236-3528-4
[1. Ravens—Fiction. 2. Toddlers—Fiction. 3. Behavior—Fiction.] I. Stucki, Ron, illustrator. II. Title.
   PZ7.A2166Ed 2014
   [E]—dc23
                                      2013027905

EDGAR
GETS READY FOR BED

BY JENNIFER ADAMS
Illustrated by Ron Stucki

GIBBS SMITH
TO ENRICH AND INSPIRE HUMANKIND

Once upon a midnight dreary . . .

"Edgar, finish your vegetables."

"NEVERMORE!"

EEEEK!

"Don't do that to your sister!"

EEEEK!

"Now go clean up your room."

"Nevermore!"

"EDGAR!"

"It's time for your bath."

"NEVERMORE!"

"Let's get you into your pajamas."

"Nebbermumble."

"Time to brush your teeth."

EEEEK!

"EDGAR!"

"Can't you sit still for one minute?"

"NO."

"Not even one?"

"NEVER."

"Come on, dear, and I'll read you a story."

"Mom, do you still love me?"

"Yes, Edgar, I'll always love you . . ."

"Evermore."